GUNFIGHT

AT

WILD RIVER

A Clay Jared Western

R. Annan

Gunfight at Wild River
Copyright 2016 by R. Annan
WGA Reg. # R31837 (4/18/2016)

Editor: Karren Doll Tolliver
Author's Portrait by Hazel Tertsakian
Photography © L. Annan

One Vision Publishing
ISBN: 978-1-942338-29-1 (e-Book)
ISBN: 978-1-942338-28-4 (Print)

Other western books by R. Annan:

Fight for the Lazy M
The Gunfighter in Winter
Long Ride to Hell's Kitchen
Owl Hawks
Gunfight at Barfield Springs
Shootout at Sanctuary City
Last Days of a Gunfighter
The Red Bandana
Copperhead Moon
Cowboys of the Box R
Prisoners of Brimstone Pass
Range War in C Minor
Devil Wind
Showdown at Wamego Falls
Lightning Riders
Winter Kill

DEDICATION

To my siblings:

Frank, Ted, George, Cyril, Gene, Herb, Jim, Dot, Ella and
Helen

1.

It had threatened rain all that day as heavy clouds churned ominously in the ugly, gray sky above. They seemed to press down on the lone rider as he made his weary way across an open field of whiskey grass to a stand of silver aspens.

The rider was a cowboy. He appeared tired and rode slowly. Hunched forward over the saddle horn, he swayed with the rhythm of the horse, trying to stay awake. At times he jerked upright with a dazed look on his face, looking around to see where he was. He often rubbed his eyes to clear the sleep out of them.

It suddenly came to him that he had wandered off the trail and was lost.

A sound like the rush of enormous wings made him turn in the saddle. The sky behind him turned black as a squall came screaming across the field in his direction. It came in sheets of needle-sharp rain, hitting him like an iron fist. The rider dropped the reins and grabbed the horn with both hands to keep from being torn from the saddle and slammed to the earth. The wind was so fierce he could barely breath against it. It almost tore the air from his lungs.

Leaning low in the saddle, he urged the animal forward toward the shelter of the trees a hundred yards ahead. The horse was frightened and complained loudly as it broke into a run.

It never saw the rock that broke its front right leg. The bone snapped loudly and the animal let out a high-pitched scream and went down sideways, taking the cowboy with it. Only luck saved him from being crushed. Even so, he went spinning to the ground, banging his head hard on the earth inches from a rock.

He lay in a daze on the ground until the cold rain snapped him back to reality. Standing up slowly, he looked around for his hat and found it several yards away. It was upside down and already half full of rain. He grabbed it, poured the water out, then put it on his head with a disgusted sigh.

The horse had gotten up, too, and was hobbling about with its ears pinned back, and its eyes rolling as it screeched out in pain. The cowboy ran up to it, grabbed the reins and brought the animal to a stop. He spoke softly to it as he dropped the saddle, saddlebags, lariat, bedroll and rifle on the ground. Finally, he removed the hackamore and tossed it down with the rest of the gear.

Both man and animal were soaked to the bone.

The cowboy laid his head against the animal's neck and spoke softly, trying to soothe and calm it down. The horse pressed its muzzle against his shoulder, listening to his voice. Man and animal held fast together as the wind and rain swept in on them with a vengeance. They seemed small and insignificant against the vast expanse of nature.

After they had clung together for a moment, the cowboy stepped back, drew his gun and shot the animal behind the ear. It turned its head and looked at him with soulful eyes, as if thankful. Seconds later, it whimpered softly, sank slowly to the earth and lay still.

Putting his gun away, the cowboy hung his head and wiped the tears and rain from his face. He knelt down, ran his hands over the animal's neck for a few moments, then stood up and looked around. Finally, picking up his gear, he walked slowly towards the stand of aspens.

The rain had slacked off now and the going was easier. There was a natural opening in the trees and the cowboy made his way through it to where it stopped. At the edge of the trees there was a long slope that led downward to a small town nestled in a U-shaped valley.

Dropping his gear, the cowboy sat on his saddle and rolled a cigarette as he studied the landscape below.

The town was at the open end of the valley, facing a river. A crude wooden bridge spanned the river, providing the only access. The U-shaped mountains surrounding the town were high and thick with pine tree growth. They formed a wall that closed the town in.

The town was active. People rode horses, drove buckboards and walked about on its main street and alleyways. All told, there were about thirty or so cabins, shacks and frame buildings. Smoke curled up from chimneys and the sounds of someone chopping wood and dogs barking drifted up on the currents.

When he was finished smoking his cigarette, the cowboy picked up his gear and started slowly down the long incline towards the river. When he reached the bottom, he stopped again to rest and take note of his surroundings.

From where he stood, the cowboy saw that a road led across the bridge, up a steep, muddy bank and into town.

Finally, he grabbed his gear again and headed for the bridge. When he got there he saw that the water was so high it lapped at the underside of the planks. Although small, the river was running so swiftly a horse could never have made it safely across. A human would be swept away like a leaf in the wind.

The cowboy crossed the bridge and stopped to look up again. He saw that the town was on a flat area above the bank. A well-worn road ran all the way up to it. He could hear the sounds of life above.

By the time he climbed up to where the road leveled off, the cowboy had to stop and rest again. He saw a stable off to his left, dragged himself slowly over to it and sat down on his saddle once more.

A bent-over, timeworn old man came out of a small shack and stood looking the cowboy over. When he saw the cowboy's sad condition he spit a spurt of tobacco juice on the ground and chuckled.

"Winded, are ya, cowboy?" the old man asked.

Too exhausted to speak, the cowboy merely nodded as he sucked in air and tried to smile at the same time.

"Where the heck did you come from?" the old man asked.

"My horse broke a leg up in the hills," the cowboy said haltingly. "You don't happen to have one for sale, do you?"

"Be glad ta sell ya one, but I don't have any."

"Anybody in town got one?" the cowboy asked.

The old man chuckled and wiped his mouth on the sleeve of his filthy cotton shirt. He sniffed to clear his nose.

"If ya want a horse here, ya gotta earn it the hard way, jest like everybody else does, sonny."

"How's that?"

"Ya gotta shoot somebody and take it!" the old man said.

At first the cowboy thought he was kidding, but the look on the old man's face said he wasn't. He was dead serious.

The cowboy looked him in the face and chuckled. "You're joshing me."

"If ya think I'm a-pullin' yer leg, then ya don't know where the heck yer at, young fellah." The old man spit another stream of tobacco juice.

"Okay, old timer, just where the heck am I?"

"Yer in Wild River now sonny, an' ya best be fast with a gun 'cause you'll be in a throw down before the day is over, and thet's fer sure."

The old man spit another stream of tobacco juice on the muddy ground and wiped his mouth on the stained sleeve of his shirt again.

"Wild River? Never heard of it," the cowboy said.

"An' thet's how we like it."

"Is there a place to eat around here?"

"Yup, Linda's Place, up the road past the Red Dog Saloon. But if I was you, I wouldn't go near the Red Dog. No sir, stay away from there. Unless ya want a throw down."

The cowboy chuckled, thinking the old man had a fixation on the throw down thing, whatever that was. Maybe he was talking about a hoedown or something.

"Can I leave my gear here, mister?" the cowboy asked.

"Sure, ifn ya got two bits."

The cowboy dug two bits from his Levi's and tossed it to the old man. It was then he noticed the sign by the shack that read: Stew Turner's Stables.

"Jest leave it over there." The old man pointed to a pile of saddles and gear under a shed.

"Keep an eye on the gear old man."

"Sure will, sonny."

The cowboy nodded and walked up the street feeling a lot lighter, but very hungry.

It was about an hour before sundown and the rain had slackened a bit. People on the street stared at the cowboy as he walked past them with his head down, plodding along, hunched over with his coat collar pulled high, his hands inside his jacket to keep off the chill.

The cowboy's mind was on his situation. He needed a horse. The old man had said he'd have to kill to get one. The cowboy chuckled. It was probably a tall tale told by a crazy old man. He sighed. His legs felt heavy. As a cowboy, he wasn't used to all this walking. He must have come two miles on foot by now. The thought of that beanery the old man talked about was the only thing keeping him going.

"Hey, you! Hold up!"

The cowboy realized he was in front of the Red Dog Saloon. It was a framed wooden structure with an open porch. Half a dozen men stood there staring down at him. Two came over to the steps. One was tall, one was shorter. They weren't dressed like working cowboys. Both wore short coats that let their guns hang free at their hips. They stared down at the cowboy with a smirk on their faces.

The cowboy stopped walking and turned around to look up at them. The tall one rudely waved the cowboy over, asking, "What's yer name, cowboy?"

"Jared. Clay Jared," the cowboy answered.

The shorter one snickered. "Well, Clay Jared, we're the Wild River Welcoming Committee and we usually collect a one-time fee from newcomers."

"I'm just passing through," Jared said. "As soon as I can get a horse, I'm leaving."

The tall one scowled. "Jest passin' through, huh? Well, passin' through or not, ya have to pay a toll."

Jared thought about the pile of saddles and gear back at the stables then suddenly realized he had stumbled into a robber's roost of some sort. Those saddles belonged to people who had wandered in and never lived long enough to leave.

And now here he was in the same situation.

2.

Clay Jared looked up at the two men staring down at him from the porch of the Red Dog Saloon, knowing they were not ordinary cowboys. At some point in time, they had given up wrangling and turned to outlaw ways. They had an aura of lawlessness about them.

A bunch of men were also standing on the porch waiting to see what would develop.

"How much is the toll?" Jared asked.

"Since you ask so many questions, it's ten double eagles fer you, friend," the tall one said with authority.

Jared sighed and looked around again. More people had gathered on the porch, several were women.

Someone said, "Looks like Sledge Bowdrie's men got themselves another pigeon!" The crowd laughed.

Another one said, "Poor sucker! He looks like he's gonna crap his pants, he's so scared." That brought more laughter.

"Maybe, maybe not. This one don't look like no pushover ta me. I think this dog has a bite!" someone else said.

"He sure is good lookin'," one of the painted ladies said.

"Yeah, I hope they don't shoot him in the face!" another replied. She smiled down at Jared.

It quickly became obvious to Jared that this was a ritual played often in Wild River, one that usually ended badly for any stranger such as he was. The crowd on the porch seemed to be enjoying Jared's discomfort, like a cat toying with a mouse.

The crowd was waiting for his fateful answer.

"Sorry," Jared finally said, "but I don't have that kind of money to waste on assholes like you two."

Without waiting for an answer, Jared walked up the street. He was about twenty feet away when the tall one shouted up at him.

"Hey! Stop, you polecat! Pay or pull!"

Jared stopped and slowly turned to stare down the road. The two men now stood in the road ten feet apart, their hands down by their guns.

"Are you two bracing me?" Jared asked.

"That's right, asshole. Pay or pull. That's how it goes in Wild River, fellah!"

"It does, huh?"

"Thet's right," the short one growled at Jared.

Jared sized them both up for a moment. Finally, he said, "Who's first?"

They looked at one another for a second and then the tall one named Pete drew without warning. His gun was halfway out of his holster when Jared's bullet slammed into his chest, knocking him flat on his back on the muddy road.

"Jesus!" someone on the porch muttered. "Did you see that? He outdrew Pete Slaughter."

The short one looked at his partner, then at Jared.

"You sonofabitch, I'm gonna kill you fer thet!"

"Kill the bastard, Ben," someone yelled from the porch. "Don't let him get away with thet!"

For a moment the short one looked down at his partner, undecided as to what to do next.

Jared re-holstered his Colt and waited, saying, "It's your call, Ben."

"Damn you, fellah!"

The man called Ben drew.

He was a little faster than his friend Pete and got a shot off. Jared had shifted to the right, went into a crouch and fanned off two shots so fast they sounded like one. The first shot took the outlaw in the chest and the second in the heart. His body twisted, jerked and slowly toppled backwards on the street. It lay there face up in the misty rain.

For a moment the crowd on the porch stood frozen and speechless, looking from Jared to the two dead gunmen and then back again.

"Christ!" someone in the crowd muttered. "He beat both Pete Slaughter and Ben Dungy! Can you believe it?

Suddenly the sound of horses came up from the bridge.

Someone yelled, "Here comes Sledge Bowdrie! Wait'll he sees what happened to his two best men!"

3.

A string of five riders came pounding up from the bridge, reined up in front of the Red Dog Saloon and stared down at the bodies of Ben Dungy and Pete Slaughter.

The leader, Sledge Bowdrie, a huge, hefty man with broad shoulders and wide around the hips was the first to slide down. He walked bowlegged over to Slaughter's body and nudged it with the toe of his worn boot.

"What the hell happened?" the big man growled at the crowd.

"It was him, Sledge," a man in a suit said, pointing at Jared.

The big outlaw turned slowly and squinted up the road. "You did this, mister?"

The cowboy nodded and said, "They braced me cold out."

The other four riders dismounted. One glared at Jared and started toward him.

"You damn polecat! Them was my pards! I'm gonna drill yer ass good!"

The big outlaw chief glanced at the man and said, "Drop it, Buck. You ain't got the spit this hombre has."

"The hell I ain't, Sledge! I'll drill his ass so fast he'll think his mammy slapped him!"

"You sure ya wanna dance with this hombre Buck?"

"I damn sure do!" Buck growled.

"Wal, okay then, it's yer funeral."

Sledge Bowdrie stepped aside and the crowd opened up. Some of them went back up on the porch, while others took to the plank sidewalks.

"Look, fellah," Jared said. "We don't have to do this. Let me buy you a drink and we'll talk it over."

"The only thing yer gonna buy is six feet a dirt!"

Buck's hand was a blur as he slapped leather. His gun came up fast and he fanned off a shot. But it was a second too late. Jared had already shot him in the heart at thirty feet away. Buck's body shuddered and his legs folded. He fell face first onto the road.

"Jesus!" Sledge Bowdrie said. He turned to one of his men. "Did you see that, Tunstall?" He had a deep-throated, grainy voice. It sounded like a bass drum with a hole torn in it.

The one called Tunstall nodded. "I sure as hell did, boss!"

The outlaw chief stared with interest at Jared. "Let's talk, cowboy."

"I'm going up to the beanery," Jared said.

"We'll go with ya," Bowdrie said, "an' I'm a-buyin'."

"Sounds good to me," Jared said.

Bowdrie pointed to a man in the crowd. "Tim, go git a buckboard an' tote these bodies over to Guthrie Jones's place fer burial. Tell him I'll settle with him later." He tossed the man a double eagle and the man ran off.

He pointed to a young boy of about fifteen.

"Bobby, you grab the reins of them three horses with the B brand on their asses an' walk them up to the bunkhouse an' feed an' water 'em. Then tie 'em in the lean-to where it's dry and rub 'em down." Bowdrie handed the boy a double eagle. The kid grabbed the reins of the horses and went up the road towards the beanery with them in tow.

Bowdrie and his three men walked up to Jared and gathered around him.

"My name is Sledge Bowdrie," the big outlaw said, "an' this is what's left of my gang, now thet you've drilled three of 'em."

"I'm Clay Jared. Sorry about that."

Bowdrie chucked. "It's okay. I ain't all thet pissed. It's what they call thet karma thing I've heard about. If it's supposed ta happen ta ya, then it'll happen." He locked his arm around Jared's and they walked up the road. As they went along, he introduced his three remaining men.

"This is Rolly Boyle, Bart Siringo an' Bob Tunstall. Thet last one ya drilled was Buck Hayden."

They stopped a moment and shook Jared's hand.

Tunstall chuckled. "Ben and Pete was playin' thet toll game agin, wasn't they?"

"Yeah," Jared said. "They wanted ten double eagles."

"Well, it sure blew up in their faces this time," Boyle said.

"I told 'em it would," Siringo cut in. "They said bullshit. I told them ta stop playin' thet game with strangers, but they jest laughed. I seen it a-comin'."

"Wal," Bowdrie added, "ya can't dodge a bullet thet has yer name writ on it. That's fer dang sure." He stared at Jared and smiled. "Hell, let's go see Linda and get somethin' ta eat. Robbin' banks sure is hard work."

It was then Jared noticed that Tunstall carried a bulging saddlebag. He thought he saw what looked like a hint of something green peeking out from under the flap, but he couldn't be sure.

They finally came to Linda's Place, a wooden structure that stood by itself about fifty yards up from the Red Dog Saloon. They could smell the pungent aroma of chili even before they got there. It was crowded inside.

Bowdrie winked at Tunstall and Siringo. The two outlaws walked off with the saddlebag while Bowdrie, Jared and Boyle went into Linda's Place. It was full.

"Wait here," Sledge Bowdrie said in his deep-throated, frog-like croak.

He walked over to a table by the window and said something to the five men sitting there. They nodded, got up and left. The old outlaw waved Jared and Boyle over with a grin. They all sat down.

"I told them fellers I'd pay their bill if they'd go down ta the Red Dog and have a drink on me," Bowdrie chuckled. "They sure liked thet idea."

"I see you have some pull around here," Jared chuckled.

"Aw, they all know ol' Sledge Bowdrie," the outlaw said modestly. "I got friends all over this here town." He paused and let his smile fade. "An' a few enemies, too."

Suddenly a pretty little Hispanic woman, looking to be in her early fifties, came over. She threw her arms around the bull-necked Bowdrie and kissed him on the cheek.

"Hola, Sledge!" Linda said. "You want chili, my love?"

"All around, little darlin'," Bowdrie said. "An' bring plenty a them tacos, too."

Linda gave Jared a look. "Where did you find this handsome hombre, Sledge?"

"He sorta dropped in," Bowdrie replied. "Sent by one of them there angels from up above." He chuckled.

Just then, Siringo and Tunstall came back without the saddlebag and sat down. They nodded knowingly to the old outlaw. Bowdrie smiled and nodded back to show he had gotten the signal.

Linda laughed, pinched Bowdrie on the left cheek and walked off into the kitchen. Bowdrie laughed, took out his tobacco pouch and started to roll a cigarette.

He stared at Jared as he worked.

"Was thet yer mount we passed up in the hills, Jared?" Bowdrie asked. Jared nodded. "What happened? A gopher hole?"

"A rock," Jared replied.

"It hurts ta put a horse down, don't it?" Boyle said.

"It sure does." Jared said seriously.

"Had him long?" Siringo asked sympathetically.

"Yeah," Jared answered. A moment later he smiled and asked, "What's the code here on gunfights?"

"Whatta ya mean?" Bowdrie asked.

"If you beat a man to the draw, do you get his outfit? Most other places you do."

Bowdrie chuckled.

"Ah, it don't work exactly like thet here," the outlaw said. "Them boys you drilled, Slaughter, Dungy an' Hayden, well, they was all ridin' my horses and rigs, too."

"Oh."

"But maybe we kin make a deal, seein' as I like you an' all, Jared," the old outlaw said.

"What sort of a deal?"

"We'll talk about it over at the Red Dog Saloon, after we eat. That is unless yer headed someplace in a hurry."

Jared chuckled. "Seeing as I'm on foot, it doesn't look like I'll be going anyplace soon."

"Where ya plannin' on sleepin' tonight?"

"I ain't figured that out yet."

It suddenly hit Jared that he was in a bad spot. No horse and no place to sleep. And outside a cold March rain was falling.

After they ate, Bowdrie paid the bill like he said he would, and they all walked down to the Red Dog Saloon.

4.

The Red Dog Saloon was very basic. It had a long, wood plank bar sitting on four empty barrels with jars and bowls of hard-boiled eggs, pickles, jerky and hardtack aligned along the front. Behind the bar was a counter with a wide selection of whiskey and locally brewed beer. Sitting behind the drinks was a huge, flaking mirror that gave a distorted reflection of the room.

The place was full with derelicts, outcasts and outlaws, not to mention card sharks and painted ladies. Cigar and cigarette smoke hung in the air, forming a thick fog under the flickering oil lamps. It swirled around the tables like the arms of a giant octopus. The heavy smell of sweat, stale tobacco juice and lamp soot lay everywhere like a moist, hot blanket.

For some of the people in the Red Dog, this was the essence of their life.

Rory Jacobs, the barman, saluted Sledge Bowdrie as he led his little band through the batwing doors. The outlaw took them to a table by the far wall. Once there he turned to Rolly Boyle.

"Go git us a bottle and some glasses, Rolly."

"Sure, boss."

"Make it two bottles."

Boyle nodded and walked out of sight towards the bar, bucking the crowd.

Bowdrie, sitting across from Jared, offered the cowboy his tobacco pouch.

"I got mine," Jared said and pulled out his own makings.

He had shown he was his own man and Bowdrie didn't like that at all. Jared had rebuffed the outlaw chief in front of his own men. Siringo and Tunstall had seen it.

"Suit yerself, Jared," Bowdrie said casually. But the look in his eyes wasn't all that friendly.

"So, what's the offer?" Jared said bluntly as he rolled a smoke. He dared not show a soft side. It would be the end of him if he did.

"You ever heard of Link Dolan?"

"Yeah, I've heard of him, why?" Jared said casually.

"Wal, he rides pretty hard here in Wild River," the old outlaw chief replied. "Not thet he's liked here much. It's more like he's got everybody buffaloed. Ya git my drift?"

"He's mean, is he?"

"Mean as a rattlesnake and shifty as a fox."

"So, what about him?"

"He and his gunnies come here when things git hot outside, like when a posse is a-runnin' up his backside."

Jared chuckled. "Sorta like you do."

Bowdrie tossed Jared a scowling look. "Yeah, sorta like I do." He wasn't smiling.

There was a moment of tension. The outlaw chief decided to let Jared's remark pass. He forced a smile.

"Anyway," Bowdrie continued, "Dolan an' me, well, we don't see eye ta eye, ya see. Ya know what I mean?"

"Sure." Jared nodded.

It was professional rivalry. He'd seen it before. Two sides fighting over territory. Life here in Wild River was close and tight. Somebody had to be the top dog. Bowdrie wanted to be that somebody and figured he needed Jared to get there.

"How do I fit in?" Jared asked. He already knew the answer, but he wanted to hear the outlaw say it.

"Wal, since you wiped out half my gang, I'd take it as a favor ifn ya did the same fer Link Dolan."

Jared thought for a moment, then said, "Your men braced me. I had no choice."

"Well, be thet as it may, as I see it, ya owes me a big favor, Jared."

Jared considered the old outlaw's demand, then came back with a counter demand of his own.

"Alright, but I'd like something in return."

"Whatta ya have in mind?"

"I want a bronc and a good one, not some broken down nag."

The outlaw chief chuckled.

"Sure" he said, "my men ride the fastest and meanest broncs ever saddled. There ain't posse nor sheriff this side a hell thet kin catch me or my men."

Jared knew he was telling the truth. A good outlaw horse could run circles around any lawman's nag.

"And one more thing," Jared said.

"Oh? An' what's thet?"

"I want five hundred a head."

The old outlaw chuckled. "What makes ya think I got thet kind a green?"

"That saddlebag Tunstall carried," Jared said. "It had a minty smell to it. It reminded me the way a bank smells."

Bowdrie laughed. "Jared, yer okay in my book. I like a fellah thet sees what's goin' on around him. Without sayin' anything more, I'll go along with thet five hundred a head."

"Shake on it?" Jared asked.

"Sure," the big man said.

He reached across the table and took Jared's smaller hand carefully in his huge, rough paw. He didn't squeeze, as expected.

"I don't want ta hurt thet hand a yers, Jared. Yer gonna be needin' it real soon." The outlaw chuckled again. He thought for a moment and added, "Where ya figurin' on stayin' ta night?"

"I haven't figured that out yet."

"Wal, how about you stay with us," the outlaw said. "We got us a nice bunkhouse out behind Linda's Place. It's best ya stay there."

"So you can keep an eye on me?" Jared added.

"Somethin' like thet," Bowdrie said. Again, he wasn't smiling when he said it. Jared had guessed right. He wanted to keep the cowboy close to his vest.

Rolly Boyle came twisting through the crowd with two bottles of rotgut. His shirt and pants pockets were full of shot glasses. Tunstall helped him set it all down on the table. Siringo poured the first round and they sat talking.

"Them banks is gettin' too damn savvy, Jared," Bowdrie said. "They're puttin' full time guards across the street ta cover the doors now."

"Yeah," Tunstall added. "An' a lot of them guards is ex-cons now workin' fer the law. Can ya beat thet?"

"It's the ranchers," Jared replied. "They got the most to lose. And with the price of beef so high now, they can afford to double up on the guards."

"Wal, it jest ain't fair," Bowdrie complained. "No, sir, it ain't fair."

"Maybe we oughta switch over ta robbin' trains, Sledge," Siringo suggested.

"I hear they're just as bad," Jared said. "They're carrying armed guards and detectives called Pinkertons."

"What the hell are Pinkertons?" Boyle chuckled. "Sounds like a bunch a girly-men ta me."

"No," Bowdrie said solemnly. "They're like bloodhounds. They git on to yer trail an' follow ya fer years until they track ya down and shoot, hang or arrest ya. An' thets a fact."

It was late and raining very hard when they left the Red Dog Saloon for the bunkhouse. They were all close to being stinking drunk. Once inside, Bowdrie pointed to the empty cots.

"Ya see them nine cots, Jared?" the outlaw said thickly, as if his tongue were swollen and dry. His short, massive legs were unsteady and he stared through half-closed eyelids. "Well, thets how many men we had. Yer lookin' at the last of the Sledge Bowdrie gang, right here. Me, Boyle, Siringo and Tunstall."

"Sorry to hear that, Bowdrie," Jared replied.

Suddenly the big outlaw started to weep. He put a massive arm around Jared and pulled him close, their heads almost touching. Bowdrie's whiskey-sodden breath was strong enough to knock over a mule.

Tunstall winked at Jared.

"The boss always gets a crying jag on when he's three sheets in tha wind."

Siringo took the old outlaw by the arm, led him back to his room in the rear of the bunkhouse and closed the door.

"Siringo is gonna make sure the boss don't hurt himself," Boyle said. "When he gits soused like this, he falls outta bed. He almost broke his neck once."

"Sure," Jared heard himself say off key.

His head was throbbing and spinning. He needed to lie down. Feeling around in the dark, he searched for an empty bunk. Finally, he found one with a pillow and a blanket and plopped down on it.

The bunkhouse kept spinning around for a while but he eventually fell asleep.

5.

They all slept late the next morning. Jared was the last one up. Bowdrie and his men watched the cowboy stagger outside, drink a gallon of water from the rain barrel and throw up. The old outlaw chuckled.

"We'll have ta find out who's makin' thet rotgut down at the Red Dog an' hang him," Bowdrie chuckled. "It sure leaves a rotten taste in yer mouth, don't it, Jared?"

Jared rubbed the sleep from his bloodshot eyes and shrugged. "Yeah, it is kinda sneaky."

A few minutes later he followed the outlaws down to Linda's Place for coffee and sinkers. After four cups of coffee he felt better.

"What you need is some hair of the dog thet bit ya, Jared," Sledge Bowdrie chuckled. He and the others seemed to be immune to the Red Dog's special brand of poison.

"No thanks," Jared said. "I've had enough of the Red Dog Saloon's cough medicine for a while."

Jared went back to the bunkhouse and lay down again.

In the middle of the afternoon Jared woke up to the echo of distant gunfire. For a moment he sat up, not sure where he was. When his mind cleared, he buckled on his gun and went outside to look around. The rain settled down to a fizzling mist so he made his way slowly along the road to Linda's Place. A bunch of customers stood on the porch staring towards the river.

Looking down the road, Jared saw people gathering on the hill above the river. He joined a small group of people heading that way and soon found Bowdrie and his men in the crowd. Everyone was staring across the river.

Far away, on the slope by the pine trees, a group of ten riders were plunging hell-bent down the long incline.

"It's Link Dolan and his men!" someone in the crowd yelled.

"Look! There's a posse comin' after them!"

A hundred yards behind them a band of fifteen horsemen came bursting out of the pine stand and down the slope in hot pursuit. Jared could hear the loud bark of gunfire and see the smoking guns. One of the outlaws slumped over his horse and slowed down.

"He's a goner!" someone yelled.

Moments later a posse-man went tumbling onto the ground as did another outlaw. The posse was slowly closing the gap. About a hundred yards from the river a third outlaw went down, and two more posse members took a dive as well.

"They're gonna make it!" someone in the crowd yelled.

The seven remaining outlaws came thundering across the bridge onto the beach area. All but one quickly dismounted with their rifles, turned their horses sideways and fired over their saddles, pouring lead into the oncoming posse.

The posse pulled right and wheeled away until they were out of range. They stopped to look back at the outlaws.

"Thet posse has had enough," Tunstall said. "They'll go home."

"Yeah, they know better than ta come in here," Siringo said. "They're finished. They'll take their dead an' go."

The posse did exactly that. They picked up their own men, the three dead outlaws and their horses and rode back up into the pines.

"How come they took Dolan's men?" Boyle asked.

"They need somethin' ta brag about and show," Bowdrie replied. "An' most likely there's a reward."

Link Dolan nodded to his men, swung into his saddle and rode slowly up the slope with them close behind. The crowd parted to let the Dolan gang pass, staring at him in awe as he went by. No one said a word. Finally, Dolan and his men stopped at the Red Dog Saloon and dismounted. The crowd followed.

It was then that Jared noticed who the rider was that hadn't dismount during the fight.

It was a girl dressed in men's clothing and her hands were tied to the saddle horn. Looking to be in her early twenties, the girl had dark red hair and a very pretty face. Her body was small but built strong. A gunbelt hung from her waist but there was no gun in the holster.

One of the outlaws walked over to her and untied her hands. She struck out at him with her fists as she unleashed a barrage of swear words that would have made the devil blush. A lucky swing caught the outlaw on the jaw, knocking him to his knees.

"Grab that wildcat, Ringo!" Dolan shouted.

Jared saw that Link Dolan was well over six feet tall. He had a large chin and a long, hawkish, pointed nose. His black eyes, set far back under his protruding forehead, matched the bushy, coal-black eyebrows and thick black hair that hung down his neck. Two of his front teeth were extra-large and pushed out against his lips, even when his mouth was closed.

The outlaw called Ringo came at the girl from the right side, grabbed the stirrup and flipped her over the left side of the saddle. When she hit the muddy street hard on her backside, the other outlaws laughed.

"Flood, you an' Potter pick the bitch up and bring her here," Dolan said as he swaggered up the porch steps of the Red Dog Saloon. "If you can't handle her, I will."

The outlaws, Django Flood and Anson Potter, grabbed the girl by the arms. She struggled to get free, kicking and twisting like a wildcat, as they dragged her up in front of their chief.

The crowd watched.

"Let me go, ya filthy coyotes!" the girl screamed.

"Shut up!" Dolan growled. The girl looked up at the menacing giant and quickly settled down. "What's your name, girl?"

"Cat Sidloe. What's it to ya!"

"Christ!" Johnny Ringo chuckled. "She's wanted as much as we are, boss!"

"Thet was my bank back there!" the girl yelled.

Dolan chuckled sarcastically. "Sure it was." He paused a moment, then growled, "Hell, girl, because of you, I lost some good men."

"I can't help it ifn we got all tangled up in a bunch. Anyway, I was inside thet bank first when you butted in. Serves ya right."

"Well, you're going to pay for the trouble you caused me, girl," Dolan replied. He looked her up and down. "One way or the other, you're gonna pay."

"I'm a girl and you can't hurt me. It's the code!"

"We'll see about that," Dolan said.

"Howdy, Dolan, long time no see!" It was Sledge Bowdrie, speaking from the bottom of the steps.

At the sound of Bowdrie's voice, Dolan gave a quick start. He turned to look down to see the old outlaw staring at up at him.

"Well, well, if it isn't Sledge Bowdrie. I thought you were dead, old man."

Boyle, Siringo and Tunstall came alongside Bowdrie. Dolan stared coldly down at them with a half a smile. The rest of his men climbed the porch steps to join him. Dolan and his five men stood smiling down at Bowdrie, Boyle, Siringo and Tunstall. Jared stood off to one side.

"Who's the little lady?" Bowdrie asked.

"If yer talkin' about me, I ain't no lady, mister. I'm Cat Sidloe, an' I'm a bank robber," the girl said.

"I'm Sledge Bowdrie, an' I heard about you," the old outlaw chuckled.

"An' I heard about you, too, Bowdrie. An' I'm darn glad ta meet ya," Cat Sidloe said.

Bart Siringo let out a scornful laugh. "Christ, what the hell is the world comin' to? Women robbin' banks! Haw!"

"Who the heck are you?" Cat Sidloe asked.

"I'm Bart Siringo, baby-doll. I hear yer fast with a gun."

"Jest give me one, an' I'll show ya how fast I am, mister."

Suddenly a cracking roar echoed up from the river. It sounded like a giant being castrated. The groaning sound went bouncing off the hills into the sky. Everyone stood still, looking at each other with raised eyebrows.

"What the hell was thet?" someone yelled.

They all turned and rushed from the saloon to the bank that led down to the river.

"Holy cow!"

"The bridge is gone!"

They all stared in shock at the sight below. A huge cottonwood had careened downstream on the raging waters and smashed into the bridge. The timbers strained and screeched out as if alive as it was torn apart at the joints. Splinters flew skyward as it burst apart and went rapidly down river, clasped in the embrace of the tree.

Everyone stood transfixed in awe of nature's wrath as tree and bridge soon became a small dot disappearing around a bend in the river.

Someone laughed sarcastically. "Well, ain't this sweet! Were stranded in this sinkin' dump now fer sure!"

The crowd milled about a while then split off into small groups of twos and threes. Some walked away alone with their heads down. Any plans of leaving Wild River had to be put on hold for now. They were all there to stay until the rain stopped and the river ebbed low, whenever that would be.

And that might not be for a long, long time.

Suddenly, Dolan yelled, "The girl! Where the hell is she?"

"She went into the Red Dog," Ronny Nelson, one of Dolan's five men, said.

"Let's go!" Dolan rushed into the Red Dog Saloon.

They found the girl at the bar stuffing hardboiled eggs and jerky into her mouth, almost swallowing it whole.

"I hope you kin pay fer thet!" Rory Jacobs, the barman, said.

"Credit?" the girl asked with a mouthful of food.

"No credit," Rory replied. "Sorry, ma'am."

Jared came up alongside the girl. He placed a double eagle on the bar in front of her. At first she didn't notice, but then she slowly realized he was standing beside her.

"You dropped this," Jared said. He laid another one down. "And this, too." He turned to Rory. "Give her a beer and anything else she wants. I'll have a beer, too."

Cat Sidloe looked Jared up and down for a moment.

"Thanks' handsome. I owe ya. What's yer handle?"

"Clay Jared."

"Yer a cowboy, aincha?"

"I sure am, Miss Sidloe."

"You follow the code?"

Jared looked into the girl's eyes. "I always have."

Rory the barman smiled and looked at Cat Sidloe.

"I'm Rory Jacobs. If yer lookin' fer a boyfriend, well, I'm available."

"Yer quite the flirt, aincha, Rory Jacobs," the girl chuckled. Jacob's face turned red.

Dolan came up alongside Jared. "You had your fun, little man. Now run along."

Jared looked up at the big outlaw and shrugged.

"I'm just standing here minding my own business. Maybe you should do the same, Dolan."

"She ain't leaving with you, if that's what you're thinking," Dolan said. "So be smart and move on."

"Let me take care of him, boss," Django Flood said. He stepped up close to Jared. They stood eye to eye. Jared backed off.

"Don't get too close, friend," Jared said.

Flood chuckled. "What's the matter? Afraid I'll try ta kiss ya, sweetie-pie?"

Half of the crowd laughed. The other half stared at Jared in silence, waiting for his reply.

"Nope. It's your breath, friend. It stinks like sheep piss."

For a moment Flood was caught off guard. He hadn't expected a counter attack. His mind raced.

"You ain't gonna stand fer thet, are ya Django?" Johnny Ringo said by way of urging his friend on. "Brace tha bastard an' drill his ass!"

"Yeah," Red Foster, another member of the gang, said. "We'll back ya!"

That was all the encouragement Django Flood needed. He sneered at Jared.

"Okay, dumbass, outside on the street!" he ordered.

"I ain't finished my beer," Jared said. "You go ahead."

"I'm bracing you, ya asshole, or are ya so stupid ya don't know it?"

"Oh, is that what you're doing? I thought you were asking me for the next dance, darling."

Cat Sidloe laughed so hard she almost choked on her food.

"Hell, Jared, give me yer gun and I'll shoot him in the balls myself!"

More laughter as Jared and Cat Sidloe smiled at each other. The fingers on Django Flood's gun hand twitched anxiously. He was hungry to make the kill.

"You done foolin' around, mister?" Flood growled

"Yep."

"Then git yer ass out on the street or I'd do ya right here an' now. Ya git me?"

"Sure," Jared said calmly. "Let's go dance."

Jared turned. His eyes narrowed and Flood could see the steel in them. The outlaw backed away for a moment. The cowboy wasn't smiling anymore.

Cat Sidloe followed Jared out the through the batwing doors into the street. Bowdrie, Tunstall, Boyle and Siringo came next. Dolan and his men were close behind them.

A crowd of townsfolk, businessmen, riffraff and painted ladies followed. They stopped on the porch to watch.

"Go up the road to Linda's Place," Jared said to Cat Sidloe.

"I ain't goin' no place. Jest give me a gun."

"No." Jared replied.

The girl stared at him. "Don't die fer me, cowboy. I ain't worth it."

Bowdrie came over to her "Don't worry about him, girl."

"Bowdrie," Link Dolan yelled. "This ain't yer affair!"

"I'm makin' it my affair, Dolan. I'm makin' sure the girl gits a fair deal!"

"So, that's how you wanna play it, do you, Bowdrie?"

"Yep. Thet's how I wanna play it, Dolan."

"I've got more guns here than you," Dolan growled. "You're a walking dead man!"

Bowdrie gave Dolan a serious look.

"Maybe we both are, Dolan. Only you don't know it!"

The girl stared at Jared with a worried look on her face.

"Go," the cowboy calmly told the girl. "We'll have a cup of coffee later."

"No, I'm stayin' right here, cowboy."

Jared looked over at Bowdrie. "Get her out of the way."

Cat Sidloe gave Jared a worried look as Bowdrie took her by the arm and pulled her to one side.

"He's gonna git kilt!" she said, almost crying.

Bowdrie chuckled. "It ain't gonna happen, baby-doll."

6.

"Kill him," Dolan said to his man Django Flood, "and be quick about it." He walked back to the porch.

Jared was standing up the street thirty feet away. Bowdrie, Siringo, Boyle and Tunstall stood off to one side, their hands on their guns, staring down at Dolan's five men. Bowdrie placed the girl behind him.

"We'll keep it fair," Bowdrie said to Jared. "You jest concentrate on what yer doing."

Jared turned his back on Django Flood for a moment and checked his gun. The outlaw stood on the road a few yards from the Red Dog Saloon, glaring up at him, anxious to get the kill over.

"Do you know who I am, fellah?" Flood called up at Jared.

"Nope," Jared answered as he turned.

"I'm Django Flood, an' I'm wanted in two states fer robbin' banks an' killin' assholes like you!"

"What's the bounty on your head, Flood?" Jared yelled back.

"Five hundred dollars!"

"Hell, that's too much." Jared replied.

"You wise-ass!" Flood screamed. "Yer gonna die!"

The outlaw drew from a crouch.

Jared read the signs and quickly shifted to Flood's right side, forcing him to turn in mid-draw. Jared's hands became a blur as he dipped low and fanned off two rapid shots so fast it sounded like one. The first bullet pounded into Flood's chest, and the second one slammed him square between the eyes. The outlaw's head snapped back, his body stiffened and he fell backwards onto the muddy street.

At that moment both sides drew, but nobody fired. It was a reflex action. Dolan nodded. He and Bowdrie put their guns away and so did the others.

"That girl belongs to me, Bowdrie!" Dolan yelled.

"We'll see," Bowdrie replied loudly. He paused a moment. "Ya best pick yer man up, Dolan. He's gettin' stiff as a board."

Dolan was twitching with anger. "This ain't over, Bowdrie. I'm coming for her and neither you nor hell can stop me!"

"Yeah? Well, I reckon I'll meet ya in hell itself someday, Dolan!" the old outlaw yelled back with a chuckle.

Dolan pointed a finger up the road at Jared.

"You just made a big mistake, cowboy. This isn't over. It's just begun. You'll be meeting some of my boys soon."

Jared ignored the threat and walked away.

Dolan turned to his men. "Take Flood to the undertakers," he shouted at them, then went up the porch steps into the Red Dog Saloon.

Ringo and Potter picked up Flood's body and tied it over his horse. Mounting their own horses, they took Flood's body down towards the river to the undertaker's place. Nelson and Foster followed Dolan into the Red Dog.

Up the street, Bowdrie complimented the cowboy.

"Nice shootin', Jared," he said, chuckling.

"What's so funny?" Jared asked.

"You. Her." The outlaw pointed at Cat Sidloe. "Whatta ya gonna do with this little hell-cat?"

"He ain't doin' nothin' with me," the girl growled. "I ain't his ta do nothing with!"

"Could Linda do something for her?" Jared asked, ignoring the girl's remark.

"Sure," Bowdrie said. "Linda an' me are close friends. She'll take care a-her."

"Dammit!" the girl said. "I don't need no takin' care of, you jackasses! All I need is a gun!"

"Can you get her a gun, Bowdrie?" Jared asked.

"Sure," the old outlaw replied. "She kin have Ben Dungy's gun. Seein' as you plugged him, he won't be needin' it no more. She kin have his pony, too, I guess." Bowdrie kept walking up the road, the others following. "You still hungry, girl?"

"Hell, yes!"

"Good. We'll fill ya up on Linda's chili. It's so hot it'll make ya grow whiskers."

The girl laughed. "The hotter the better, mister."

Half an hour later they sat in Linda's Place watching Cat Sidloe eat her second bowl of chili. Jared and the others were on their second cup of coffee.

"How'd ya git mixed up in this business, girl?" Bowdrie asked Sidloe.

She looked up from her bowl of chili and gave the question some thought. Finally, she spoke.

"I did it first ta save the ranch in Montana," she said. "Then, when my mom got sick real bad, I did it ta pay fer her doctor bills. The third time I did it ta buy a weddin' dress, but the sonofabitch ran out on me."

"Yer a long way from home," Boyle said.

"What about the fourth time?" Bowdrie asked.

"I did it the fourth time because I was bored as hell," the girl replied with a chuckle. She looked over at Jared as he rolled a cigarette. "You don't talk much, do ya, Jared?"

Bart Siringo snickered. "He's in love with ya and he's all tongue-tied, is what."

Rolly Boyle and Bob Tunstall chortled over that remark.

"Well, he sure pulled my bacon outta the fire," Cat Sidloe replied. "An' I won't fergit that."

Jared gave the girl a serious look.

"You should go back to that farm in Montana," Jared said. "Get married and raise kids."

"Shucks! I'm too wild fer thet now."

"You're sure a wild one, alright, Miss Sidloe, ma'am," Rolly Boyle said.

Old Bowdrie looked thoughtful. "You sorta remind me of my Mary. She passed on some years back. Caught the fever. She was wild same as you are. Pretty as a picture, too.

As his eyes turned wet, he pulled a bandana out of his back pocket and blew his nose.

They were all quiet out of respect for the old outlaw's loss. He finally smiled and called Linda over.

"Howdy, lover," Linda said. "Who's thet ya got there, yer daughter?"

"No, but she's a good friend a mine an' the boys, Linda, my love. She'll be needin' a place ta stay. Kin' ya do thet? I'll square it with ya."

"Sure," Linda replied lightly. "I'll take her under my wing fer ya, darlin'. But when are ya gonna make an honest woman of me, huh?"

The old outlaw blushed a little. "Now, you stop thet, girl. People will start talkin', by golly!"

Everyone laughed. Linda went back into the kitchen.

"She sure nailed you, boss!" Bob Tunstall said.

"I reckon she did, Bob," Bowdrie admitted. "I reckon she did."

Later they left Cat Sidloe with Linda and walked over to the bunkhouse. Once there, Bowdrie went into the back room. Five minutes later he came out and gave Jared the five hundred dollars he had promised.

"Thet was neat shootin', Jared," Bowdrie said. "Thet's one down."

That night, as he lay on his cot, Jared thought about the girl, Cat Sidloe. She had asked him if he was a cowboy of the code and he had said he was. She had reached out to him in her need for help. Under all that bravado he sensed she was really frightened.

He also thought about Sledge Bowdrie, a man of the Old West. For him too, the code still existed. He had gone out of his way to help the girl. But for Link Dolan, the code meant nothing. His loyalties only reached as far as himself and his men. Everything outside his narrow circle was fair game.

As he lay there thinking, Jared wondered if he would ever get out of Wild River alive. Dolan would be sending men to kill him. The odds were, he would one day be found lying face down in the mud with a bullet in his heart and it would all be legal and up front.

A duel to the death. Two men with guns, facing off to see who was the fastest. And it would happen out on the streets of Wild River, in shootout after shootout, until Clay Jared was dead.

Dolan would make sure that it happened that way and Jared was helpless to stop him.

There was no way out for the cowboy. Absolutely no way out.

7.

Jared got up early the next day and went outside. There was a basin on a small washstand with a mirror above it. He wiped the rain off the mirror, looked at his image and groaned.

"You look like crap, Jared," Siringo said as he came out.

"Yeah," Jared said. "I didn't sleep so good last night."

The washbasin was full of very cold rain water. Jared splashed some on his face to wake up, then used his bandana to dry off.

Bowdrie came out yawning. He nodded to Jared.

"You look like crap, Jared," he remarked.

Jared shrugged and replied. "Yeah, so I've been told."

Boyle and Tunstall appeared, stretching and shivering. They looked at Jared.

"I know," Jared said. "I look like crap. It's already been said twice."

The outlaws laughed.

"Come on," Bowdrie said. "Let's go see Linda fer some flapjacks and molasses."

They walked down the road together. When they got to Linda's Place, Jared kept going on down the road.

"Where ya goin', Jared?" Bowdrie called after him.

"Down to the stable," Jared called back. "Gotta get my saddle and gear before they start to rot! I'll meet you at Linda's."

It took Jared an hour to walk down to the stable, grab his gear, tote it back to the bunkhouse and go back to Linda's Place. By then he was hungry as a bear. He ordered ham, eggs, grits and coffee and finished them off quickly.

"Where's the girl?" Jared asked after he had eaten.

At that moment Cat Sidloe came out of the kitchen wearing an apron. She came over to the table.

"How'd ya like them ham, eggs an' grits, Jared?"

"Mighty fine."

"Well, I cooked it."

"No!" Jared pretended to be surprised.

"I sure did."

Bowdrie sniffed for attention. "Is Linda treatin' ya right, girl?"

"She sure is. She's jest great. Like a momma ta me."

"Well, you let ol' Sledge know if ya need anything," Bowdrie said. "Anything at all."

"I sure will, Bowdrie."

The girl looked at Jared for a moment then went back into the kitchen.

"Did ya git yer gear?" Bowdrie asked Jared.

"Yep. Got it all. All I need is a bronc."

The old outlaw nodded. "Wal, I suppose ya kin use the one I lent Buck Hayden, since ya done drilled him, too. It's jest sittin' out there in the lean-to waitin' ta be rid."

"Which one is it?" Jared asked.

"It's the bay mustang."

Tunstall chuckled. "Ya best be careful around thet bay mustang, Jared."

"Oh? How come?"

Bart Siringo cut in. "Because thet bay is as cold-backed an' ornery as a thick-headed mule. He won't roll on ya, but he'll try ta swap ends with ya until he gits warmed up."

Boyle added, "He ain't the fastest bronc, but he'll keep a goin' until the sun sets an' rises agin in the mornin'."

"It's as fine an outlaw horse as you'll every throw a saddle on, Jared," Bowdrie said. "An' thet's no lie."

At that moment someone shouted outside in front of the beanery.

"Hey, Jared! You in there, you polecat? Come on out!"

"Oh, oh!" Tunstall said. "The throw down is a startin'."

Jared stood up and checked his gun.

"You want some back-up?" Siringo asked.

"If there's more than two, I'll give a yell," Jared replied.

He glanced at Bowdrie and walked outside. It was raining again, a fine misty drizzle that drifted about on the breeze.

Dolan's man, Johnny Ringo, stood in the street. His wide-brimmed black hat sparkled with the fine rain that fell. Jared remembered seeing him hanging around Link Dolan and his men. Ringo was calm and sure of himself. He had a cigarette in his mouth, but tossed it away when Jared walked out on the street.

He was wearing a pair of fine, new kidskin gloves. Jared saw the gloves and smiled.

"What's your name?" Jared asked.

"Ringo. Johnny Ringo."

Jared stepped down off the porch into the street.

"What do you want with me, Ringo?"

"Take a guess, friend."

Jared smiled and nodded. "Because I drilled Django Flood?"

"Yep. See, yer not as stupid as they say ya are cowboy."

Jared looked up at the sky. The clouds were dark gray and seemed low enough to reach up and touch.

"This ain't a good day for this, friend," Jared said. "Can't we do it some other time, when the weather is better?"

"The boss wants it done now," Ringo said, smiling. "So, here I am."

Jared smiled back. "Yep. So, here you are, doing what your boss says to do."

"Thet's right, doing what I do best."

Jared sighed. "You're a good man, Ringo. Too bad we can't be friends."

"I don't see how thet could happen now, Jared."

"Yeah. I guess you're right. Too bad, though."

Nothing more needed to be said. Dolan wanted him dead and had sent his best man to do the job. It was that simple.

Jared turned his back on Ringo and walked slowly up the street, putting more distance between the two. The outlaw watched him. His eyes never lost sight of Jared.

"Thet'll do it!" Ringo called out. "Right about there!"

But Jared didn't stop at Ringo's pleasure. He walked five more paces up the road, putting more distance between the two.

"I said stop, ya sonofabitch!"

Jared turned. It was raining harder now. The figure down the road was but a dull silhouette. Jared could not see

Ringo's eyes. Only those nice, new, soft, yellow kidskin gloves that Ringo wore.

Jared knew they were soaking up the rain.

"I guess this is it, Ringo," Jared said. "So long, friend."

"We ain't friends," Ringo growled.

Both men drew at the same time. Ringo tried to fan off a shot, but the glove on his left hand slowed him down. It caught on the hammer and threw his aim off. Jared felt the heat of the bullet as it sped past his neck, giving it a quick burn.

Jared's left hand, slick from the rain, danced over the hammer of his Colt four times. Two of those four bullets hit Ringo dead center in the chest. He grunted from the impact and sat down in the road. He tried to raise his gun, but it suddenly felt too heavy. He dropped it, folded over on his face in the muddy street and died.

Jared walked slowly towards Ringo's body, reloading his Colt as he went. He saw Link Dolan come out of the Red Dog Saloon further down the road. Potter, Nelson and Foster were with him.

"He was a good man, Dolan!" Jared yelled out in the rain. "The next time do your own dirty work, ya yellow bellied skunk!"

He stared at Johnny Ringo, shook his head, reloaded his gun and went up the porch steps into Linda's Place. When they came out an hour later to go up to the bunkhouse, they saw that Ringo's body was gone. Once inside the bunkhouse, Bowdrie took Jared aside and paid him another five hundred dollars. The cowboy wondered where the old outlaw was getting the money from and decided it was from that saddlebag he had seen stuffed with money from the bank they had robbed just before coming to Wild River.

"How much for Dolan?" the old outlaw asked.

"You can have him dead in the street for free," Jared muttered.

There was something about Johnny Ringo that reminded him of someone he'd met long ago. Jared almost felt as if he had killed an old friend.

8.

It continued to rain hard enough to keep the river at flood level. Sometimes a tree or large stump would rush down from upstream and go past the town, rolling, tumbling and bobbing up and down. When a bush snagged a rock, it would hang there until a larger piece of debris smashed into it, breaking it loose. Then both would go flying down the river together.

The day after the Ringo throw down, a lone rider dressed in black rode fast out of the woods and down the slope to the edge of the river. He stood on the far bank looking over his shoulder from time to time. Finally, he fired his gun in the air to get the attention of a cowboy on the hill. The cowboy walked down to see him.

"Whatta you want, mister?"

"Is Link Dolan around?"

"Yeah, why?"

"Tell him that Ace Latimer wants to see him."

"Sure. Throw me over a double eagle."

The man threw a double eagle across to the cowboy.

The cowboy, who knew Dolan, ran up to the Red Dog Saloon to deliver the message. In twenty minutes, Dolan, Potter, Nelson and Foster came down to the edge of the river. Dolan waved across at the man.

"Hi, Ace! Long time no see. What's up?"

"I got a posse about an hour behind me," Latimer yelled back.

"That's too bad, Ace. It really is." Dolan said with a smirk.

"Come on, Dolan, throw me a rope."

"I will, for fifty percent."

"Okay, but hurry!" Latimer yelled against the wind.

The outlaw waited as Dolan sent Potter up to the mercantile to buy a rope. He soon came back with it and handed it to Red Foster. Foster tied a rock around one end, swung it like a lasso and sent it sailing across the river. On the first two tries, it fell short. On the third one, it made it. Latimer tied it around a boulder near the water's edge while Potter tied his end high on the trunk of a tall pine tree.

Latimer reached into his saddlebag and pulled out wads of money, which he stuffed into his shirt, pants and coat pockets. He dropped the rest of his gear on the road and slapped his horse on the rump. At first it was confused, not knowing what to do, but it finally ran up the bank into the pine trees.

The outlaw stood staring at the fifty-foot wide span of roiling water for a moment and then walked in, grabbing the rope. The current caught his body at the legs and tried to pull him downstream, but he managed to hold on. Placing one hand over the other, Latimer inched his way slowly across the river.

It was exhausting work and midway he began to slow down. A wad of bills fell out of his back pocket and scattered on the wind like tiny, green birds. Most of it settled down and was carried away by the water. Those on the bank could hear him cursing.

Finally, he was back in shallow water and was able to pull himself up on the shore. He was soaked from the legs down, and his boots made a squishing sound when he walked.

He cut the end of the rope with his boot knife and it snapped away into the river.

"Thet's two double eagles for the rope," Potter said. "It's on you."

"Sure," Latimer said.

He fished the money out of his pants pocket and gave it to Potter then walked up the street into town. The crowd walked behind.

Latimer led his followers up to the Red Dog Saloon. He sat on the porch, emptied the water from his boots and went inside to treat himself and everybody to a bottle of rotgut.

He stood at the bar smiling, a tall, slim, handsome man in his thirties who looked more like a bank executive or a lawyer than an outlaw. His face was clean and smooth, with a thin, attractive mustache about his upper lip. He was a man who always hid his true feelings behind a provocative, suggestive smile designed to appeal to women.

His clothing was not that of a cowboy or even an outlaw. He was dressed in city clothes, with a black Stetson, a dark brown tweed suit with a short coat and vest. A single-action Colt in a black leather holster hung on his hip.

At the first chance, Dolan took Latimer aside out of earshot of the others.

"About that fifty percent, Latimer," Dolan said. "You can keep it. Me and my boys got plenty from the Benton Springs job we just pulled. But maybe you can help me with a little problem I have."

"Sure, what is it?"

"You remember Sledge Bowdrie?"

"Sure, but I heard he was dead."

"Not hardly. He's living right here in Wild River."

"What about him?"

"He's sitting on eighty thousand he took from the bank in Sterling," Dolan said, knowing it was a lie.

Latimer looked impressed.

"How many men has he got?"

"That's where you come in," Dolan said. "Bowdrie's only got himself, three men and a drifter named Clay Jared."

"And you?"

"I've got myself, Nelson, Potter and Foster."

"He's one man up on you," Latimer said.

"Yeah, but not if you throw in with me."

Latimer nodded, pulled his pouch out of his vest and started rolling a cigarette.

"What have you got in mind, Dolan?"

"Him and his men got a place up in back of Linda's beanery," Dolan explained. "Some night, when they're all drunk and asleep, we could ambush them. Kill them all and take the money. How does that sound to you?"

Latimer lit his cigarette and nodded, pretending to mull it over. He knew it wasn't about the money.

"We could do that, Link," Latimer said. "Or we could do something else."

"Like what?"

"Like have some fun. I could brace the old fart and kill him. After that, his men would either scatter or join up with you, since you're low on men."

Dolan thought about that and nodded.

"Alright. We could try that." He paused a moment. "When would you brace him?"

Latimer chuckled. "Relax. I'll pick a time and place. He ain't going anywhere and neither are we with the bridge out."

"Yeah, you're right, there. Nobody's leaving for a while," Dolan said. He suddenly looked serious. "But There's something else I'd like done before you brace Bowdrie."

"Yeah? What's that?"

"There's that drifter I mentioned."

"What about him?"

"I want him taken down first, and down real hard."

Latimer stared at Dolan and noticed the fire of hate burning in his eyes.

"That sounds personal, Dolan. What's the cowboy done to you?"

"He took down two of my best men, Ringo and Flood," Dolan growled. "I want that bastard dead."

Latimer sipped his glass of whiskey and took a pull on his cigarette.

"That's a personal problem."

"You won't kill him for me?"

Latimer didn't blink when he said, "Like I said, it's a personal problem. I don't do personal problems."

Suddenly Link Dolan got angry. He wanted that meddling cowboy Jared and Sledge Bowdrie out of the way so that the path would be open to teach that snotty little bitch, Cat Sidloe, a lesson she'd never forget.

"Fine," Dolan finally conceded. "I'll get someone else to do it, then. Nelson should be able to do it. He's fast as greased lightning."

Latimer shrugged and nodded, "Sure. You do that."

Latimer's mind was turning things over. This was beginning to look like a grudge war between the Dolan and Bowdrie gangs. He wasn't sure which side he wanted to be on just yet. He'd have to examine it closer, see what was what and who was who.

Then he'd make a final decision.

9.

Word soon reached Sledge Bowdrie that Dolan had gotten reinforcements in the form of bank robber and fast gun Jack "Ace" Latimer. He gathered Boyle, Siringo, Tunstall and Jared in the bunkhouse to talk about the situation.

"I know about this Ace Latimer hombre," Bowdrie said. "He's got quite a reputation as a fast draw."

"I heard he took down Roscoe Gandy over in Abilene last year," Tunstall said. "Seems like they fought over a girl."

"I heard thet it was over a horse," Boyle cut in.

"Whatever," Tunstall replied. "Anybody who could beat Roscoe Gandy on the draw is pretty damn fast."

"Where's he from?" Bowdrie wondered aloud.

"I heard he's from Texas," Siringo replied. "From down around the Nueces River area, near Corpus Christi."

"I wonder how he got across the river?" Bowdrie asked.

Boyle replied, "Someone threw a rope across to him."

"It was most likely Dolan, seein' how Latimer is talkin' with him," Siringo said.

"Wal, if he's from Texas, then maybe he's got a little code in him," Bowdrie muttered. "Then, agin, maybe not."

A few hours later, they went down to Linda's Place for an evening bowl of chili. As they sat there eating and smoking, Ace Latimer came in. He stood at the door, looking around with confidence.

Bowdrie glanced towards the doorway and said, "Looky there. Thet's a gunslinger if I ever saw one."

Latimer's gaze fastened on Bowdrie and his men. Adjusting his gunbelt, he then sauntered casually over to an adjacent table. He sat down with his back to them.

Bowdrie stared at the back of Latimer's head for a moment.

"Are you Bowdrie?" Latimer asked without turning.

"Yeah, I'm Bowdrie. What about it?"

"Dolan told me a lot about you."

"You must be Latimer, then."

Latimer nodded. "Yeah, that's me. Women call me Jack and men call me Ace."

"Well, Ace, I heard you threw in with thet skunk, Dolan," Bowdrie said.

"Is that what you heard, Bowdrie?"

"Yeah, thets what I heard, Latimer."

"And if I did?"

"Then yer makin' a big mistake."

"I'd say that remains to be seen, doesn't it?"

"How much is he payin' ya, Latimer?"

"I don't need any money. I have plenty of my own," Latimer said. "But just so you know, he's after that eighty thousand you got from the job in Sterling."

Bowdrie laughed hard for a moment.

"What's so funny?" Latimer asked.

"Thet's the first lie Dolan told ya. There ain't no eighty thousand. We only got thirty thousand."

"Oh? And what's the other lie?"

"He ain't after the money. He's after the girl!"

Latimer slowly turned around in his chair. He fastened his eyes on Jared for a second, then turned to Bowdrie.

"Girl?" He frowned. "What girl?"

"He didn't tell you about the girl?" Bowdrie asked.

"No. Suppose you tell me about the girl, Bowdrie."

"Sure. Be glad to. Her name is Cat Sidloe. She crossed Dolan up, so he brought her here ta take it out on her. An' he woulda, exceptin' Jared here plugged Django Flood and saved her."

Latimer looked at Jared and chuckled.

"I guess you're the cowboy Dolan is so mad about."

"An' Jared here killed Dolan's man, Johnny Ringo, too," Boyle boasted. "Dolan is scared pink of Jared."

Ace Latimer looked Jared up and down. Jared ignored him.

"They say you're pretty fast for a cowboy. Is that true?" he asked.

Jared only shrugged and sipped his cup of coffee.

"I see you're the quiet type," Latimer went on. "I like that in a man. I never trust a man who talks too much."

Jared said nothing and started rolling a cigarette.

Suddenly Linda came over from where she had been talking to some men at the counter.

"Ready to order, mister?"

"I'll have a bowl of your finest chili, ma'am," Latimer said charmingly. He added, "And coffee, if you please, ma'am."

"Well, well, he's not only handsome, but he's a gentleman, too," Linda said, smiling at Latimer.

After Linda left for the kitchen, the gunslinger stared at Jared.

"Dolan wanted me to brace you, Jared."

Jared shrugged and looked down at his coffee cup. "Thanks for the warning, Latimer. When do we do it?"

"There's no rush," Latimer replied. "Unless you're in a big hurry." He paused a moment. "Anyway, I said I wasn't interested in killing any cowboys."

"If you change your mind, Latimer, let me know," Jared said as he lit his cigarette. "And don't send somebody to call me out. Tell it to my face."

Latimer smiled. "I always do, Jared. I always do."

"Good," Jared replied casually. "I appreciate that."

Cat Sidloe came out of the kitchen carrying a tray with Latimer's bowl of chili, some tacos and a cup of coffee on it. When she saw Latimer, she froze in place for a moment then quickly recovered and set the tray down in front of him. Her eyes locked with Latimer's and held.

Bowdrie, Jared and the others noticed the immediate attraction between Latimer and Cat Sidloe. It was intense, like a lightning strike. Latimer's face went soft and a big smile broke out.

Cat was the first to speak.

"Linda said ya was a good looker," she said. Her eyes took a quick survey of the handsome gunman. It was plain to see she was fascinated by him. "An', by golly, she was right. Where ya been all my life, handsome?"

For a moment, the outlaw was speechless. He stared into her eyes, a big smile on his face. Finally, he broke the silence.

"Where have I been? Why, I've been looking all over the world for you," Latimer said sweetly. "And it looks like I've finally found you, darling."

For a moment Cat Sidloe didn't know what to say to this slick-talking man.

"Enjoy yer chili," was all she could manage. She started to turn away and head for the kitchen but stopped. Latimer had hold of one of her hands.

"What's your name, sweetheart?"

Suddenly Bowdrie said, "Don't let him slick talk ya, girl. He's workin' fer thet skunk, Dolan!"

The words hit Cat Sidloe like a hammer. She pulled her hand away and stepped back, glaring at Latimer.

"It thet true?"

"It was, a while ago," Latimer said. "But not anymore."

"What's yer name, mister?" Cat growled angrily.

"Ace Latimer. You can call me Jack."

"Well, Mister Ace Latimer, you better get out of here," Cat Sidloe said, as she rushed back into the kitchen.

For a moment no one spoke. They stared at Latimer as if he were something curious. There was a subtle change in him, as if the wind had gone out of his sails. He stared at the kitchen door where the girl had disappeared.

The others watched in silent curiosity while he ate his food. When he was finished, he turned to Bowdrie.

"Is it true, what you said about her and Dolan?"

"Yep! Jest ask Jared here, or any of the others. They'll tell you it's true, Latimer."

Latimer rubbed his neck for a moment and nodded. He believed it was true. He had seen the girl. Finally, he sighed, stood up and came around to face Jared.

"One of Dolan's men will be coming after you, Jared," Latimer said. "A man named Nelson. Ronny Nelson."

"Never heard of him," Jared said casually.

"I have. When you face him, don't blink or you'll be dead. He's one of the fastest around."

Latimer dropped six bits on his table. He looked towards the kitchen door once more and left.

"Damn," Bart Siringo said. "Thet gal turned his head so fast it made me dizzy!"

"She sure did, alright," old Bowdrie chuckled. "She surely did. It was a wonder to behold."

They all laughed.

10.

Several days slid by. Things had quieted down and there were no killings. Then it started again.

It was another rainy day in Wild River and Clay Jared sat alone in Linda's Place drinking coffee. Bowdrie, Boyle, Tunstall and Siringo were in the bunkhouse playing cards. Five minutes ago an old man had come and told the cowboy that Ronny Nelson was waiting for him out in front of the Red Dog Saloon. This Nelson wanted to brace Jared.

Jared purposely took his time and ordered another cup of coffee. Inwardly, he was sick of killing and he was wondering when his luck would run out. He knew that being fast on the draw wasn't enough. To stay alive, he had to think ahead, to read the other man's mind. Guessing wouldn't always work. Nelson would be doing the same to him.

The old man came back a second time. He looked afraid.

"Tell him I'm coming," Jared said with a heavy sigh.

After the old man left, he stood up and checked his gun again like he had done not more than ten minutes ago. Cat Sidloe and Linda came over to him. The young girl put a hand on his shoulder. She was on the edge of crying.

"I'll go back ta Dolan if thet will stop the killin'."

"No, it won't. Once he's finished with all of us, he'll come for you," Jared said wearily. "I saw it in his eyes. He's dirty and evil."

Linda looked sad. "All this killin' has ta stop. It jest has ta stop!"

"It won't stop as long as Dolan is here," Jared said.

He went outside into a fine rain and stood on the porch of the beanery, looking down the road. Ronny Nelson was on the porch of the Red Dog Saloon. When he saw Jared, he stepped down into the road and took up the stance. He seemed anxious to get it over.

"Git yer stinkin' ass down here, cowboy!" Nelson yelled up the road. He was very confident and this worried Jared.

Jared deliberately moved slow, taking his time walking off the porch and getting in position out on the road. A large crowd had braved the elements and was standing on the saloon porch, staring up at him. Dolan was next to Anson Potter and Red Foster, the only other ones left in his gang besides Nelson. Jared didn't see Latimer there.

"Come on, you slow sonofabitch! I ain't got all day!" Nelson was angry. A cowboy was making him wait. No bronc-busting cow puncher had the right to do that.

Jared finally stopped forty feet or so away and waited. Nelson didn't like that distance so he closed the gap another ten feet and took up the stance again. Jared smiled and backed away an equal distance.

"What the hell you doin'?" Nelson asked. "Stop runnin' away, ya damn fool!"

"I gotta," Jared yelled. "Your breath is making me sick. It smells like you've been kissing a pig, Nelson."

Nelson began trembling with rage at the insult.

"Before I kill you, ya Jared. I want ya ta know I ran with Billy the Kid. How's thet grab ya?"

Jared yelled back, over the wind and the rain. "You probably polished his boots and kissed his ass!"

"Ya smart-ass egg sucker, jest fer that I'm gonna shoot ya in the mouth!" The outlaw's body was shaking. "I'm gonna kill ya, you piss-ant!"

Nelson struck quickly and without warning. Jared reacted by going into a crouch and drawing as fast as he could. He fanned off three shots, not realizing that Nelson had already got off two bullets. One took Jared's hat off and the other cut a path across his left temple. Nelson had gambled on a head shot and almost pulled it off.

Jared felt dizzy and nauseous for a moment. He couldn't focus his eyes and realized he was losing his footing. The world went spinning around him. Blood ran warm down the side of his head. He waited for Nelson's next fusillade of bullets, but it never came.

The next thing Jared knew Siringo and Tunstall had him by the arms and were dragging him up the road towards the beanery.

"I guess I missed," Jared muttered almost as if drunk.

"The hell you did, Jared," he heard Boyle say. "You drilled Nelson two outta three!"

"I did?"

"Damn if ya didn't, cowboy!" Tunstall chuckled.

"My hat!"

"I got it!" Boyle said.

They hustled Jared into Linda's Place and sat him in a chair. When Linda saw him she whined and ran into the kitchen.

Sledge Bowdrie came over to examine Jared's head.

"How'd it go?" he asked his men.

"Nelson's done fer, boss," Siringo chuckled. "Jared put three lead pills in his ass."

Linda returned with a basin of warm water and some towels. Cat Sidloe and Ace Latimer came out with her. They watched as Linda went to work on Jared's head.

"Is he hurt bad?" Cat Sidloe asked.

"Bad enough," Linda said as she cleaned the side of Jared's face, "but he'll be okay."

A man came into Linda's Place and stood in the doorway. He waited until someone noticed he was there.

'Whatta ya want, Fred?" Siringo asked.

"Nelson's pard, Red Foster, wants a crack at the cowboy," Fred said. "He's a-waitin' out by the Red Dog Saloon."

For a moment no one spoke. Bowdrie looked at Siringo, Siringo looked at Boyle and Boyle looked at Tunstall.

"Hell," Tunstall said. "I'll go out."

"I've got this one," Latimer said as he checked his Colt. "Foster and I don't see eye to eye anyway, so it's time we settled."

Cat Sidloe grabbed Latimer's hand. "Don't go out there, Jack. It's a trap."

"I'll be fine, Catherine," Latimer replied. He kissed her on the cheek and followed Fred out the door.

"Should we back him up, boss?" Siringo asked Bowdrie. "It might be an ambush."

The old outlaw nodded. "Hell, why not. Sure."

Bowdrie, Boyle, Tunstall and Siringo walked outside.

When they got to the street they saw Red Foster and Ace Latimer were already lined up facing each other about thirty feet apart. Latimer was taking his time getting into place.

Dolan's other man, Anson Potter, suddenly stepped down into the road alongside Foster, catching Latimer off guard, making it two against one.

"One of you go even it up," Bowdrie said quickly.

"I'll go," Siringo said. "I never liked Potter."

Bart Siringo walked down onto the road and stood a few feet from Latimer, facing Potter.

"Hope ya don't mind me joinin' the party, Latimer."

Latimer smiled. "No. I was just going to yell for help anyway."

Red Foster yelled up the road at Latimer.

"Whatta you buttin' in fer, Latimer? I'm after Jared, not you."

"You'll have to settle with me, Red," Latimer yelled.

Anson Potter scowled up at Siringo. "An' what the hell are you doin' here, Siringo?"

"I'm jest here ta even things up," Siringo yelled back. "An seein' as I don't like yer funky ass, I'm gonna drill ya."

Suddenly Dolan hollered, "Latimer! You double-crossing rat! I should have known I couldn't trust you."

"If you want the girl, Dolan, you'll have to come through me to get her!" Latimer yelled.

Dolan laughed loudly. "Okay, so I didn't tell you about the girl. So what? She's a sneaking little rat and I'll fix her one way or the other, even if I have to do it myself."

The other people on the porch with Dolan stepped back in the shadows to watch from a safer spot.

Dolan roared at Potter and Foster. "Kill them, boys!"

The barking of four guns split the cold, rainy air, bounced off the buildings and echoed down the riverbank and across the field into the pines. Even the slow downpour of rain was unable to stop the roaring sound.

Bart Siringo and Ace Latimer dipped low and rolled sideways as they fanned of five shots each at Potter and Foster. Dolan's men met shot for shot, firing back up the road with nerves of steel.

Siringo was the first to go down, not all the way, but on his knees, with a bullet in one leg and another low on his left side. Latimer's hat lay twenty feet in back of him in the mud, and he had taken a bullet high on the outside of his shoulder.

Potter stood grinning, not realizing he was dead, with a bullet in his heart and stomach. Finally, he fell forward on his face in the road. Foster was down with two bullets in his chest and one between his eyes.

"You okay, Siringo?" Latimer asked, reloading. He put his gun away and went to help Siringo up on his feet.

"I'm getting' rusty as an' ol' barn gate," Siringo groaned in pain.

Siringo held onto Latimer as the two went up the road to Linda's Place. Latimer scooped his hat up on the way.

Link Dolan stood stone-faced on the porch staring at the bodies of the last of his gang. He had ridden into Wild River with good men, all fast on the draw. Men who obeyed his every command. Now they were all dead. Every single one of them.

The big outlaw stood on the porch of the Red Dog Saloon and stared up at Linda's Place with clenched teeth and tight jaws.

"You're all dead," he growled. "You don't know it yet, but you're all dead!"

Dolan walked over to his room in the flea-bitten place known as the Palace Hotel and sat on his cot drinking from a bottle of rotgut. He was all alone now. For the first time in his life, Dolan had no one to bark demands at or order around.

He laughed to himself. He would fix things. Get things back to normal. Wild River was infested with the lowest forms of humanity that ever walked on two feet.

Men who had committed every kind of crime imaginable, some too horrible to mention, skulked about the back alleys of Wild River. There was a whole subculture out there waiting for a leader. All it took to buy their services, if not their loyalty, was money.

Link Dolan had plenty of money, since he no longer had anyone to share it with.

"You're all dead!" he muttered as he tossed down a shot of red eye. "You're all dead! And the girl is mine!"

11.

The day after the last shootout, Link Dolan sat alone in his dingy, stuffy, foul-smelling room in the Palace Hotel smoking and drinking. He was also thinking.

Now that his gang had been wiped out in gun duels with Bowdrie's men, Link Dolan was sitting on the money from the Benton Springs robbery. It was all his own now, with no one to share it with. Dolan was trying to think of a way to use some of it to get revenge on the Bowdrie gang, the girl and the cowboy Clay Jared.

In Wild River nothing mattered except money. Money could buy anything in a place where life was cheap.

Dolan scowled as he sat there filled with hate. He was especially angry at Latimer. He would have to die for siding with Bowdrie and the girl. Oh, yes! He must be made to regret that decision. Killing Latimer was on the top of Dolan's list.

Link Dolan finally came up with a plan and began putting the first stage into play right away. He used the rumor mill in Wild River to get the message going around that he'd pay top dollar to anyone who was willing to join his new gang. The only requirement was to follow orders and not ask questions.

In less than a week Dolan made contact with six of Wild River's meanest cutthroats. They met in the Red Dog Saloon for a talk. All of them were outside of the law, dodging the hangman's noose for one reason or another, but mostly for cold-blooded murder. Since Wild River had a woman shortage, just the mention of Cat Sidloe being fair game made their mouths water. She was a prize worth fighting for.

Even without that incentive, these men were filled with anger and frustration from being stuck like prisoners in Wild River. They dared not go out into the world again for fear of being hunted down like the animals they were.

Knowing their situation, Link Dolan was just the man to manipulate their primitive energy and get it to strike where he wanted it to.

He also sold them on the dream of getting their freedom back. With him as their leader, they would ride again as they did in the old days, fast and free. A promise he knew he could never keep, nor did he have any intention of keeping.

His object was to use these men and leave them high and dry the first chance he got.

Dolan gathered his cohorts at a table in a far, dark corner of the Red Dog Saloon to lay out his plan. He provided plenty of whiskey and food. He let them indulge themselves for a while, waiting for the right moment to jump in and reveal his plan. It soon came.

"Men," Dolan said, "here's the deal. Sledge Bowdrie is sitting on a pile of money that he and his boys got from robbing the bank in Sterling. All we have to do it go over there and take it away from him."

He waited until his words sunk into their thick skulls.

"How much has Bowdrie got?" one of them finally asked.

He was taller and meaner looking than all the others. His name was Cal and he seemed to be the self-elected leader of this band of misfits.

Dolan hesitated for a moment, searching his mind for a figure large enough to capture their interest.

"Seventy thousand," he replied. "That will give us about ten thousand each, at least."

He waited to see their reaction.

"I dunno," another said, "ol' Sledge, he's pretty fast with a gun. An' so is Siringo, Boyle and Tunstall, not ta mention thet cowboy, Jared."

"I see your point," Dolan replied. "But we won't be bracing Bowdrie and his men in the open. No, what we'll do is catch them sleeping. We'll set their place on fire and shoot them as they come running out. It's as easy as that."

It was a simple, safe plan that Dolan knew would appeal to cowards and murderers such as they were. He purposely didn't mention Ace Latimer.

Another outlaw said, "I'd feel better if Bowdrie was outta the picture. He's one mean hombre."

Dolan nodded, stalling for a moment, trying to come up with a reply that would appeal to them.

"Alright. What if I took care of Bowdrie myself? Would that do it, if I took him out?"

"Maybe," another said, looking around at the others.

There was another moment of tension before they all nodded. Dolan sighed with relief. He had them with him again.

"What if we did pull it off," Cal said, "what good would it do us? We're still stuck here. We can't leave."

The others saw the logic in this. Freedom was an elusive bird always out of reach. Again, Dolan had to think fast for words to convince them he had their best interests at heart.

"How would you men like to be back in business again?" he asked.

"Whatta ya mean?" Cal questioned.

"As soon as the rain stops, the river will go down fast. How would you men like to ride out of here with me and hit the bank at Ferris Landing?"

"We don't have horses," Cal said.

Dolan chuckled.

"There are plenty of empty saddles to go around. I know of at least six. And after Bowdrie and his men are out of the way, there'll be more. You can have their guns, too. Hell, you can have everything they've got!'

They looked around at each other, smiling and nodding. Dolan saw that he had them completely now.

Cal said, "Man, it sure would feel good ta have a horse under me agin an' ride hell-bent-fer-leather with a saddlebag full of cash!" He nodded at his fellow cohorts. "I'd head fer Mexico and buy me a hacienda an' a pretty senorita, by golly!"

They all nodded at Cal's imagined dream.

"An' yer gonna take care of Bowdrie?" one asked again, just to make sure he understood.

"Yep," Dolan replied. "I'll take care of Bowdrie."

"When?" another asked.

"He'll be dead before sundown tomorrow," Dolan boasted.

Suddenly, one of them chuckled sarcastically, "Hell, it ain't gonna stop rainin' fer another month, at least."

"Yeah," another agreed. "It ain't never gonna stop rainin'."

That seemed to put a damper on Dolan's plans.

Suddenly a strange thing happened. The doorway of the Red Dog Saloon began to glow with a strange light. It got brighter and brighter, as if the street was on fire. It got so bright it hurt the eyes of the men inside, making them squint and rub their eyes.

"Good God Almighty!" Rory Jacobs, the barman, yelled. "The sun is out! It's stopped raining!"

Those inside the Red Dog Saloon could hear people out in the street shouting and laughing. Dogs were barking. They could hear guns roaring as people fired them in celebration.

Dolan smiled. He had pulled it off.

Bowdrie, his men and that cowboy Jared would soon be dead. All he would have to do then was to hold onto the girl, wait for the river to go down and ride out on the sly before Cal and those idiots realized he was gone.

They'd have their money, horses and guns. Cal would take charge and they would go on robbing banks as they did before coming to Wild River. Then Dolan would take Cat Sidloe with him into the hills of Montana.

But what about Latimer? Suddenly Link realized he would have to kill Latimer or he'd never be able to get at Cat Sidloe. That might mean killing Linda as well.

12.

Jared and Bowdrie sat in Linda's Place talking over an afternoon cup of coffee. Linda came over to tease the old outlaw as she often did.

"When are ya gonna make an honest woman of me, Bowdrie?"

The old outlaw chuckled. "I don't know what yer talkin' about, little darlin'," Sledge said, his face growing red.

"Sure ya do. Ya promised ta take me away from all this, remember?"

Linda Garner had been in Wild River since it was a mining camp, years ago. After the gold ran out, some people had put down roots and stayed. A lot of the sodbusters, pig and sheep farmers, sellers of merchandise and booze, stablemen and blacksmiths had decided to stay put. The town had nearly everything except a church, a pastor and a marshal.

One pastor had come but didn't fare very well. There was just too much drinking and killing going on as outlaws turned Wild River into a sanctuary, a refuge from the long arm of the law. If anyone in Wild River prayed, they did so in dark, quiet places so that no one heard them but God. Or they would go to the next town, ten miles upriver, and pray at the church there.

As for the law in Wild River, since they couldn't get a marshal to stay, the town had its own form of citizen's justice. Townspeople and business people came together to apply the rope or the rifle to those who went too far. In this respect, the outlaws were far outnumbered and had to be careful where they tread. Many saw their friends dance from the end of a rope. It was a constant reminder of who really owned Wild River.

As for the business people of Wild River, they took the money of good and bad people alike and never judged where it came from. It was better not to get involved with the subculture, the dirty unwashed.

That was also Linda's motto. Don't stick your nose where it don't belong. But Sledge Bowdrie and his friends were the one exception. The old-fashioned outlaw was her favorite customer. He was easygoing, generous and kind. She never tired of making him blush with her kidding around.

"Anytime ya wanna give up robbin' banks, Sledge, you and me kin connect as partners, if ya want," Linda said. "Ya know I got a thing fer big, handsome outlaws like you!"

Perhaps she wasn't kidding. Sledge never knew, but he liked to hear her say it, even if he didn't take it seriously.

Sunlight lit up Linda's Place. It felt like a heavy weight had been lifted from the town. People walked around smiling. The road was hard and dry for the first time in months.

A man appeared in the doorway of Linda's Place and looked around as his eyes adjusted to the change in light. When he saw Jared and Bowdrie he spoke.

"Mr. Bowdrie, Mr. Dolan is waitin' fer you out front of the Red Dog Saloon, sir."

"What was thet, Bob?" Bowdrie asked.

"I said, Mr. Dolan sent me ta say he's waitin' fer you out front of the Red Dog Saloon. An' ta make sure ya come alone with a gun."

"Alright, Bob," Bowdrie said. "Tell him I'm comin' as soon as I finish my coffee." The man didn't move so Bowdrie asked, "Anything else, Bob?"

"Mr. Dolan said ta give me a double eagle, Mr. Bowdrie."

Sledge Bowdrie frowned. "He said thet, did he?"

"Yes, sir, Mr. Bowdrie. Thet's what he said, alright."

Bowdrie chuckled, dug a double eagle out of his pants pocket and tossed it across the room to Bob. It went past him and into the street. He ran after it.

Linda looked concerned. "Don't go out there, Sledge!"

"He has to go, Linda," Jared said. "You know that."

Bowdrie pulled his big frame up from his chair and adjusted his gunbelt. He opened the gate of his Colt and carefully checked the load. Satisfied, he snapped it shut and put the gun back in his holster. He smiled down at Linda. She was crying.

"I'll be right back fer another cup a coffee, little lady," the outlaw said, smiling. He adjusted his hat and bandana. Linda came up to him and buttoned the top button of his worn flannel shirt.

"You look a mess," she said nervously.

"Wait'll ya see Dolan when I'm finished wif him," Bowdrie chuckled nervously.

"Go with him, Jared!" Linda said urgently. "Back him up!"

Jared nodded and walked outside with Bowdrie. A crowd had gathered on the plank sidewalks and the porches along the street. Word had spread quickly about what was commonly called, in Wild River, a throw down. It was a term that had caught on long ago and stuck. It sounded adventurous and dangerous.

Dolan was out in front of the Red Dog Saloon, waiting anxiously for Bowdrie.

"Come on, you old fart!" Dolan yelled to the delight of the crowd on the saloon porch. "Come meet your maker!"

Bowdrie took his time. He walked towards Dolan, picked his spot and stopped. He adjusted his gunbelt again.

"You gonna bark or are ya gonna bite?" Bowdrie yelled down at Dolan.

"You in a hurry to die, old man?"

"I got better things ta do than spend time with a back-stabbin' polecat like you, Dolan. So, let's dance!"

Dolan chuckled. "Sure, old man! Here it comes!"

A second before Link Dolan drew, a gun blasted from somewhere. A bullet hit Sledge Bowdrie in the chest and staggered him. Dolan's gun came up a split second later and he shot the old outlaw in the heart.

A third gun roared, and Jared saw a man with a rifle jerk and fall off the roof of a building next to the Red Dog Saloon. He landed in the street with a crunching thud. Ace Latimer came walking out of the shadows across the street, holstering his Colt.

Jared cleared the porch steps of Linda's Place in one leap. As he hit the road, he drew his gun.

Dolan was gone.

Linda came running out of the beanery into the road. She rushed to Bowdrie and knelt at his side.

"You darn old fool!" Her tears fell on Bowdrie's face. "I told ya not ta go!"

Bowdrie coughed. Blood bubbled from the corner of his mouth. "You ain't cryin' fer ol' Sledge, now, are ya?"

"Yes, you old fool, I am."

Bowdrie forced a smile. "Shucks, thet's the nicest thing," Bowdrie said. He closed his eyes with a deep sigh and stopped breathing. Linda looked up, her face a mask of grief.

"He's gone now. Sledge Bowdrie is gone." She looked at Jared. "Kill Dolan for me, won't ya, Jared?"

Linda got up and walked slowly back to the beanery. Jared looked up toward the bunkhouse, wondering why Boyle, Tunstall and Siringo hadn't come out.

Latimer came walking up the road.

"Who was that on the roof?" Jared asked.

"A man named Tom," Latimer said. "He was one of the six men Dolan hired."

Suddenly gunfire sounded. Jared wasn't sure where it came from. It sounded like it was coming from up the road, near Linda's Place. There were only three shots and then silence.

"Somebody is hunting in the woods," a member of the crowd said.

At that moment, Linda rushed out of her place.

"She's gone! Dolan took her!" she screamed. "Thet skunk took Cat!"

Jared and Latimer ran up the road. Some of the crowd followed. Linda had a bruise on the side of her jaw. She leaned against the building for support. Latimer held her.

"What happened?" Latimer asked.

"Thet sidewinder Dolan hit me an' took her!"

Jared ran toward the bunkhouse. When he got there he drew his gun and rushed in.

Boyle, Siringo and Tunstall lay dead on the floor with their guns still in their holsters.

They had been ambushed.

13.

Link Dolan's plan was to draw attention to the throw down between himself and Sledge Bowdrie. To make sure he came out on top, he had put the man called Tom up on the roof of the building next to the Red Dog Saloon with a rifle.

"When you see me start to draw, you kill the old bastard." Dolan had instructed. "You got that?"

"Sure, I got it," Tom had said confidently.

While this was going on, Cal and the other men in his gang would be up behind Bowdrie's bunkhouse, waiting. When they heard the first shot, they were to rush in and catch Bowdrie's men by surprise.

Dolan had told them, "Kill whoever is in there. Then find the money and come back here."

The plan worked well except that the murderers didn't find the money. Being born liars themselves, they assumed that Dolan had lied to them.

After they had killed Boyle, Tunstall and Siringo, the men searched high and low but they didn't find the saddlebag full of money that Dolan said would be there. When they heard someone coming, they ran away into the woods and cut back to the Red Dog Saloon to confront Dolan.

When they got there, they saw Dolan holding a young girl by the arm and began to suspect his true motive. He had used them for his own purpose.

"There weren't no money there," Cal blurted out. He stood close to Dolan, staring at Cat Sidloe. "We didn't find a damn cent there!"

Dolan twisted Cat's arm as she tried to break away from him.

"He's only using you," she growled. "Can't ya see thet?"

Dolan slapped her hard across the face, jolting her into silence.

One of the men said angrily, "There wasn't nothin' said about no girl, either, Dolan! What the hell is she doin' here?"

"She's my girl," Dolan said, smiling. "You know how women are. You have to put them in their place every once in a while."

"No, she ain't," another one said. "She's the one thet Jared took away from you. I saw it happen."

Dolan looked over at Cal for help. Cal stared blankly back. For all their trouble, they hadn't gotten the seventy thousand dollars Dolan said they would get. Not a damn, red cent. Cal was not a happy man.

Dolan suddenly realized his plans were unraveling. He looked towards the door of the saloon and saw a crowd had gathered on the street. Latimer stood on the porch staring in at him.

"Send the girl out, Dolan," Latimer yelled, "and maybe I won't kill you."

Suddenly, all the customers in the saloon walked quickly outside with their hands held high. Once on the street, they ran for cover.

Moments later, Jared shouted, "We've got twenty guns out here, Dolan! You don't stand a chance!"

When Dolan heard this, he turned to Cal and said, "Put half your men on the back door in case they try to rush us!"

Cal sent two men to guard the back door. The remaining two stood near him.

"What's the next move?" Cal asked Dolan.

"I don't know! Let me think!" Dolan let go of Cat's arm and went to the bar. "Give me a whiskey! And hurry it up!" he growled at Rory Jacobs.

The two men near Cal didn't look too happy.

One said, "This asshole has got us up a tree, Cal."

"There's only two ways outta here," the other one said, "an' thets out the front or the back. An' I ain't one fer runnin' out the back like a cornered rat."

Cal nodded and called his men together for a powwow. Dolan and Cat Sidloe watched, wondering what was going to happen.

"Fellahs, it's time ta separate the men from the boys. What's it gonna be?" Cal asked.

"Heck," one of them said, "They're gonna hang us fer bushwhackin' Boyle, Siringo an' Tunstall anyway, so let's show 'em what we're made of!"

"Hell yeah!" another said and let out with a high-pitched rebel yell.

"Then, let's do it!" Cal growled.

Cal and his men shook hands, slapped each other on the back and said goodbye. Finally, they lined up side by side, facing the batwing doors.

"Let it rip!" Cal screamed.

They pulled their guns and hit the door on the run. All five outlaws were met with a rain of bullets. Some stray rounds tore chunks out of the doors and hit the ceiling inside. Cat and Dolan crouched low. The shooting lasted less than a minute and then all went quiet.

Dolan grabbed Cat Sidloe by the arm. He was dragging her towards the back door when Jared and Latimer came in the front with their guns drawn.

"Hold it, Dolan!" Latimer yelled.

For a second Dolan froze, then quickly reacted. He spun Cat Sidloe around in front of him using her as a shield, pointing his gun at her head.

"Drop your guns or she's dead!" Dolan shouted.

"You'll never make it out of here alive," Jared said. "Let her go and you and I will settle it outside. One on one."

"I'll count to three and I'll kill her!" Dolan yelled.

"Okay, okay," Latimer said. He put his gun down on the floor. Jared did the same.

"What's the next move, Dolan?" Jared asked.

"He's a coward," Latimer scowled. "He hides behind women."

"Yeah," Jared said. "He ain't half the man Sledge Bowdrie was."

Jared could see Dolan's face turning purple with anger.

"He's a sissy-boy," Jared said.

"Yeah," Latimer said.

"I'm gonna kick his ass," Jared said and started to walk towards Dolan.

"You're dead, Jared!" Dolan screamed.

The outlaw shoved Cat Sidloe aside and turned his gun on Jared.

"Hey, asshole!" Rory Jacobs yelled.

He pulled the trigger on the scattergun he had gotten from beneath the bar. The full blast of the twenty-gauge shell smashed into Dolan's chest and sent him flying across the room. His body crashed against the wall and he slid down into a sitting position. He had an odd smile on his face, as if he were thinking about something funny.

"That was for Sledge Bowdrie," Rory said, reloading the scattergun.

For a moment, Cat Sidloe, Latimer and Jared held their ears in pain. Finally, Latimer and Jared picked up their guns. Cat Sidloe rushed into Latimer's arms.

"Are you okay, Cat?" Latimer asked.

"I'm fine."

People started peeking in through the door.

"Come on in," Rory Jacobs hollered. "The bar is open." Then he added. "Will somebody drag thet body out of here before it starts stinkin' up the place? Whoever does it gets a free drink."

Two men grabbed Dolan's body by the feet and dragged him out and down to the undertaker's place.

14.

Linda had a special headstone made for Sledge Bowdrie's grave in the cemetery on a hill near a stand of whispering pines behind the town. She found time each day to pick wildflowers and put them at the base of the cross there.

The sun came out every day and the river quickly went down. Soon it settled down to its usual smoothness and was shallow enough to walk a horse across to the other side. The bridge was still gone, but nobody seemed in a big hurry to build a new one.

The first to leave were Cat Sidloe and Ace Latimer.

They had found Dolan's money up in his room under the floorboards at the Palace Hotel where he had squirreled it away so no one could find it. No one except Ace Latimer and Cat Sidloe. They could smell money a mile away. With both Dolan's money and Latimer's, they had two saddlebags full of green stuff.

Jared was in Linda's Place when Latimer and Cat came to say adios. They rode two of the horses that once belonged to Dolan's men. It seemed there were plenty of empty saddles in Wild River now that the two outlaw gangs were dead.

"Where are you headed?" Linda asked.

"We're headed fer Texas," Cat said.

"We're gonna buy a saloon and name it the Wild River Saloon," Latimer said.

"No fooling?" Jared asked.

"Yep," Cat replied. "Goin' to El Paso. No one knows us there." She paused a moment, then added, "An' if they do, why we'll just ride over ta Juarez an' start agin."

Jared and Linda walked down to the slope and watched with sadness as Jack "Ace" Latimer and Catherine "Cat" Sidloe rode slowly across Wild River. Once they were on the other side the two stopped to wave back at them. After that, they rode quickly on into the pines, out of sight.

Jared and Linda went back to the beanery and sat at a table talking over a cup of coffee.

Linda laughed and said, "It won't last."

"Why not?" Jared asked. "They're in love. Or at least it looks that way to me."

"He's a lover. He draws women like honey draws flies," Linda smiled. "She'll either shoot him or leave him. No, it won't last long. She shoulda chose you, Jared."

"No," he said. "I've got no urge to put down roots just yet."

A few days later, a sheriff came into Wild River with a large posse looking for the Bowdrie and the Dolan gangs. After looking around, the posse did some serious drinking at the Red Dog Saloon and left. They never thought to check the graveyard out back in the field by the whispering pines.

After they were gone, Jared laughed to himself.

"What's so funny," Linda asked.

"They'll be a long time looking for those two gangs," Jared said. "Maybe we should have told them where they are."

One thing bothered Jared. If no one had found the money Bowdrie's gang had gotten from the Sterling robbery, where was it? Did Linda know where it was? Did she have it? Was the money still hidden somewhere near the bunkhouse? And how much was it, really?

The answers came one day when Jared was about to leave Wild River. He had saddled up the bay mustang that Bowdrie had given him. For a packhorse he had chosen Tunstall's appaloosa, a big, sturdy animal.

He figured on packing up a two-week supply of food and feed for the horses. He would head for Caldwell, far to the south, near the Texas border. He'd heard of a big spread down there that was always hiring. It would be good to get back doing what he loved best, riding for the brand.

At the time it happened, he was in the lean-to filling two saddlebags with grain, using a tin coffee cup to dip up the oats stored there. Suddenly he hit something solid buried deep in the grain barrel. Reaching in with one hand, he felt around and discovered the saddlebag filled with money from the Sterling robbery.

After thinking about what to do with it, he wrapped it in a burlap sack and put it in the backpack on the appaloosa.

That day, around noon, he had his last bowl of chili at Linda's Place.

"So, yer finally leaving Linda high and dry, are ya, handsome?"

Linda stared hard at the cowboy's face, studying it closely so she wouldn't forget it.

Jared nodded. "Yep. I just remembered I'm still a cowboy. I almost forgot, for a while."

Linda got up on her toes and kissed Jared on the cheek.

"I'll miss the heck outta ya, Jared," she said, sniffing back her tears. "Whenever I think of ol' Sledge and the boys, I'll think of you, too. An' I hope ya don't you forget ol' Linda, as well. You're gonna be a legend here in Wild River."

Jared smiled. "Every bowl of chili I have, for the rest of my life, will make me think of you, sweetheart."

"Aw, get goin' before I start blubberin'."

Jared bent, kissed her on the cheek, walked outside and mounted up.

With the appaloosa's reins tied to the saddle of the mustang, he rode gently along the street of town, taking a last look. A few people waved goodbye as he headed down the slope and across the river. Once on the other side, he stopped for a minute to roll a cigarette. As he smoked, he looked up at the town of Wild River. When the cigarette was finished, he rode on.

...

Two days later Jared rode into the cattle depot of Sterling, Kansas. He rode across the train tracks and stopped to ask a woman where the bank was. She gave him a very suspicious look and turned away without answering him. Farther up the road he asked a young boy the same question.

"It straight up the road, mister," the boy said. "Are ya gonna rob it?"

"Why, you wanna help?"

The boy's eyes grew big. "Sure, kin I?"

"How come you're not in school?" Jared asked.

"It's none a yer business, mister," the boy said and ran up an alley.

Jared tied up in front of the only bank in Sterling and walked in. A clerk at a desk looked at his dusty, travel-worn clothes and then ignored him. Jared walked over and stood in line at a teller's cage.

"Can I help you, sir?" the woman teller asked.

"I'd like to see the manager, ma'am."

"He's very busy, sir," she said, staring at his dusty hat. "Perhaps I can take care of you."

She was very pretty and Jared chuckled as a thought came into his mind.

"Did I say something to amuse you, sir?"

"No, ma'am," Jared replied.

"Just what did you want to see the manager about?"

"About a bank robbery."

Suddenly the woman in line behind Jared screamed. "It's a robbery!" She ran out of the bank.

The teller in the next cage looked frightened. "Don't hurt me! How much do you want?"

Suddenly Jared found himself surrounded by four men with guns. He held up his hands.

"I just wanted to see the manager is all," Jared said.

They took his Colt and hustled him into a back room. A few minutes later a distinguished man with gray hair wearing glasses came in.

"Who are you?"

"I'm Clay Jared." Realizing his situation, Jared added, "I'm a bounty hunter."

"What do you want?"

"I don't want anything. I was just passing through and thought you'd like to have the money back."

"What money?"

"The thirty thousand the Bowdrie gang took from you a while back."

"You have it?

"Sure. It's in a sack on that packhorse tied outside."

"I'll go check, sir," one of the armed men said and left.

"How did you get the money," the manager asked.

"I tracked Bowdrie to Wild River and found where he had stashed it." Jared paused a second. "I understand there's a reward?"

"If what you say is true, yes, there is."

"How much?"

"Five hundred dollars."

Jared suppressed a grin. Moments later the man came back with the saddlebag and put it on the desk. The manager opened it and dumped the money out. He and a clerk began to count it. Fifteen minutes later, he turned to Jared smiling.

"Is it all there, sir?" Jared asked.

"It seems to be."

Jared knew it was. He had counted it and added all the money that Bowdrie had given him for killing Dolan's men. He didn't want dirty money. He wanted to be able to sleep nights.

"The customers and shareholders of the Sterling Savings and Loan are most thankful to you, Mr. Jared," the manager said. He turned to the clerk. "Draw up a draft for five hundred dollars to Mr. Jared."

Jared cleared his throat. "I'd rather have cash. In hundreds, if it's alright."

"As you wish, Mr. Jared."

"And may I have my gun back, sir?"

"Of course."

Half an hour later, after signing a receipt, Jared was on his way out of town with five hundred dollars in his shirt pocket. That was over two years' pay for a cowboy.

"Thanks, Sledge, old man," he chuckled. "I owe you."

Jared rode out of town and slowly followed the road out of Sterling. About ten miles from town, he came to a crossroad that led north and south. He stopped, wrapped a leg around the saddle horn and rolled a cigarette.

Looking up at the sky he saw an eagle high above, wheeling about against a bank of clouds painted orange by the setting sun. Jared stared at it as it grew smaller and smaller. Finally, it was but a tiny speck on the horizon and then nothing at all.

When his cigarette was finished, Jared patted his horse on the neck, spoke soothingly to it and rode south. He figured on stopping at the first cattle town he came to, to see who was hiring. The call of the bunkhouse and the friendships that went with it were too strong to break.

He was a cowboy and would always be one.

The End

A Note from the Author

Thank you for reading my book. Would you please consider rating and reviewing it? I'd enjoy your feedback. Thank you!

Western Books by R. Annan

Fight for the Lazy M

The Gunfighter in Winter

Long Ride to Hell's Kitchen

Owl Hawks

Gunfight at Barfield Springs

Shootout at Sanctuary City

Last Days of a Gunfighter

The Red Bandana

Copperhead Moon

Cowboys of the Box R

Prisoners of Brimstone Pass

Range War in C Minor

Devil Wind

Showdown at Wamego Falls

Lightning Riders

Winter Kill

Look for other western books to appear soon.

About the Author

R. Annan is a well-traveled author with many interests. As a career serviceman, he served in Korea and Vietnam. He also completed a one-year course at the Defense Language Institute in Monterey, California, and graduated from the University of South Florida with a B.A. in Art and Art History. After taking a two-year course in screenwriting at the Hollywood Scriptwriting Institute, he established The Old Time Radio Club Time Machine as both a scriptwriter and an actor.

As a young boy growing up in the city, R. Annan never passed up a chance to see a western movie. His heroes were Buck Jones, Johnny Mack Brown, Wild Bill Elliot and John Wayne, to name a few. As an adult, he often wondered where his love of westerns came from. Perhaps it has something to do with his grandfather, John L. Annan, who was a cowboy from Helena, Montana, in days of old.

www.ingramcontent.com/pod-product-compliance
Lightning Source LLC
Chambersburg PA
CBHW060632130626
46555CB00002B/760